My Babies, My Tw

Big Sister

Story and Art by

Vivian Caldwell

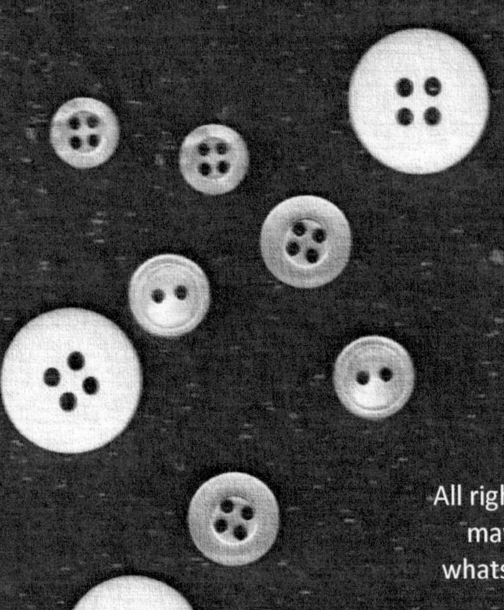

Story and Art by Vivian Caldwell

For further inquiries please contact the author at

www.viviancaldwell.com

ISBN-13: 978-1523604999

ISBN-10: 1523604999

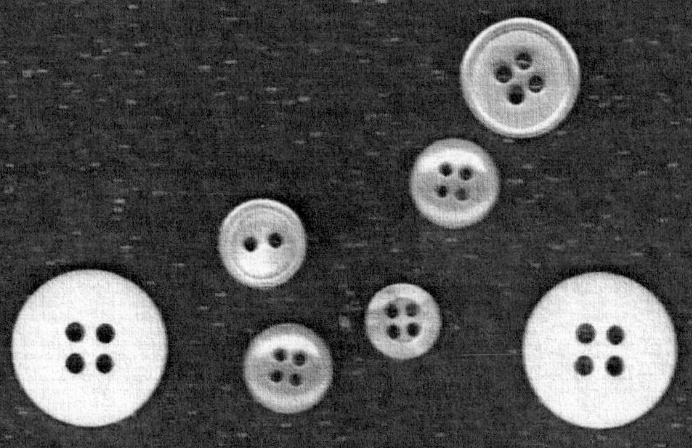

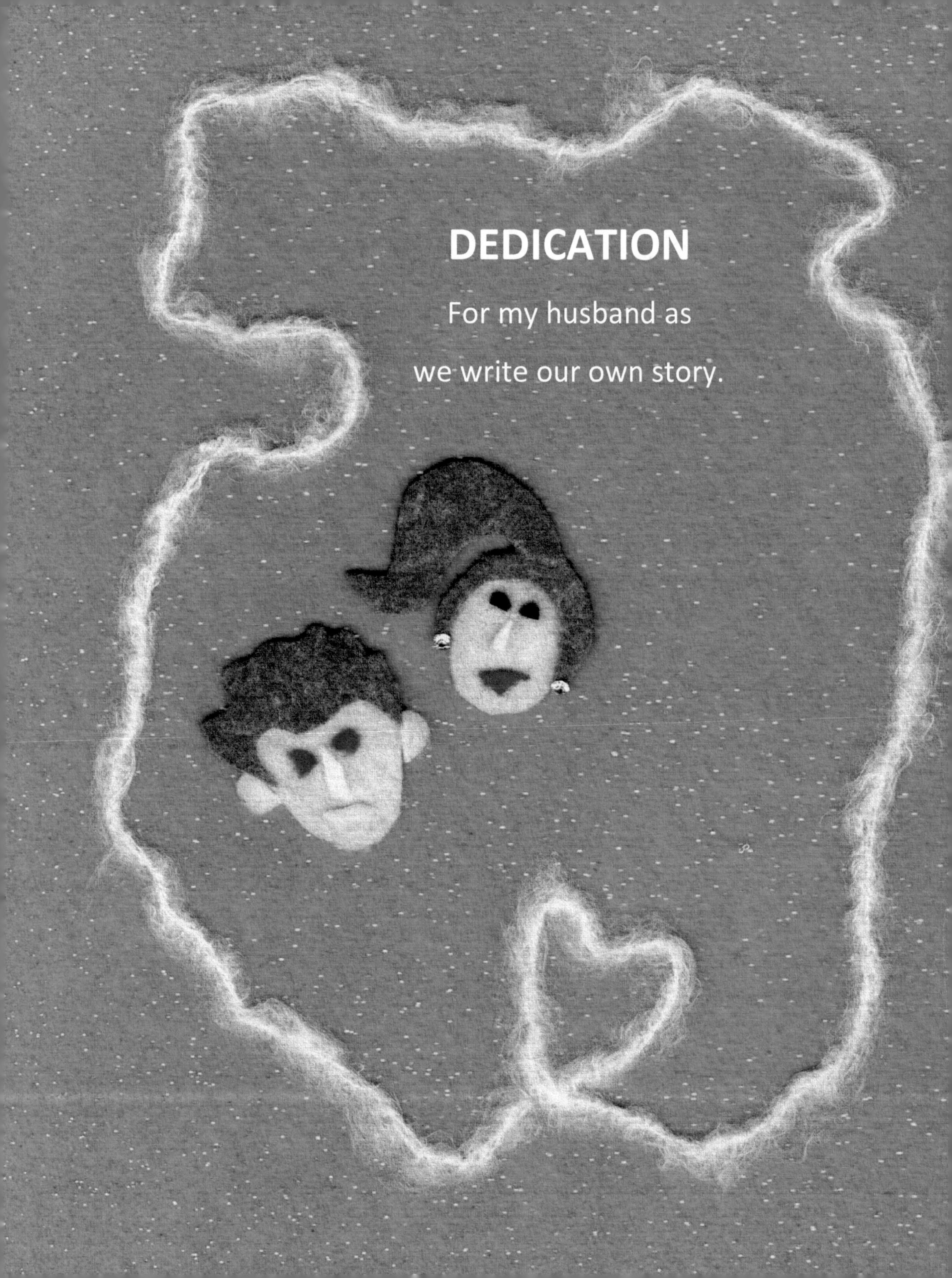

DEDICATION

For my husband as

we write our own story.

Grandma and Daddy are saying,

two babies will make three;

I see Mommy sitting and I climb upon her knee.

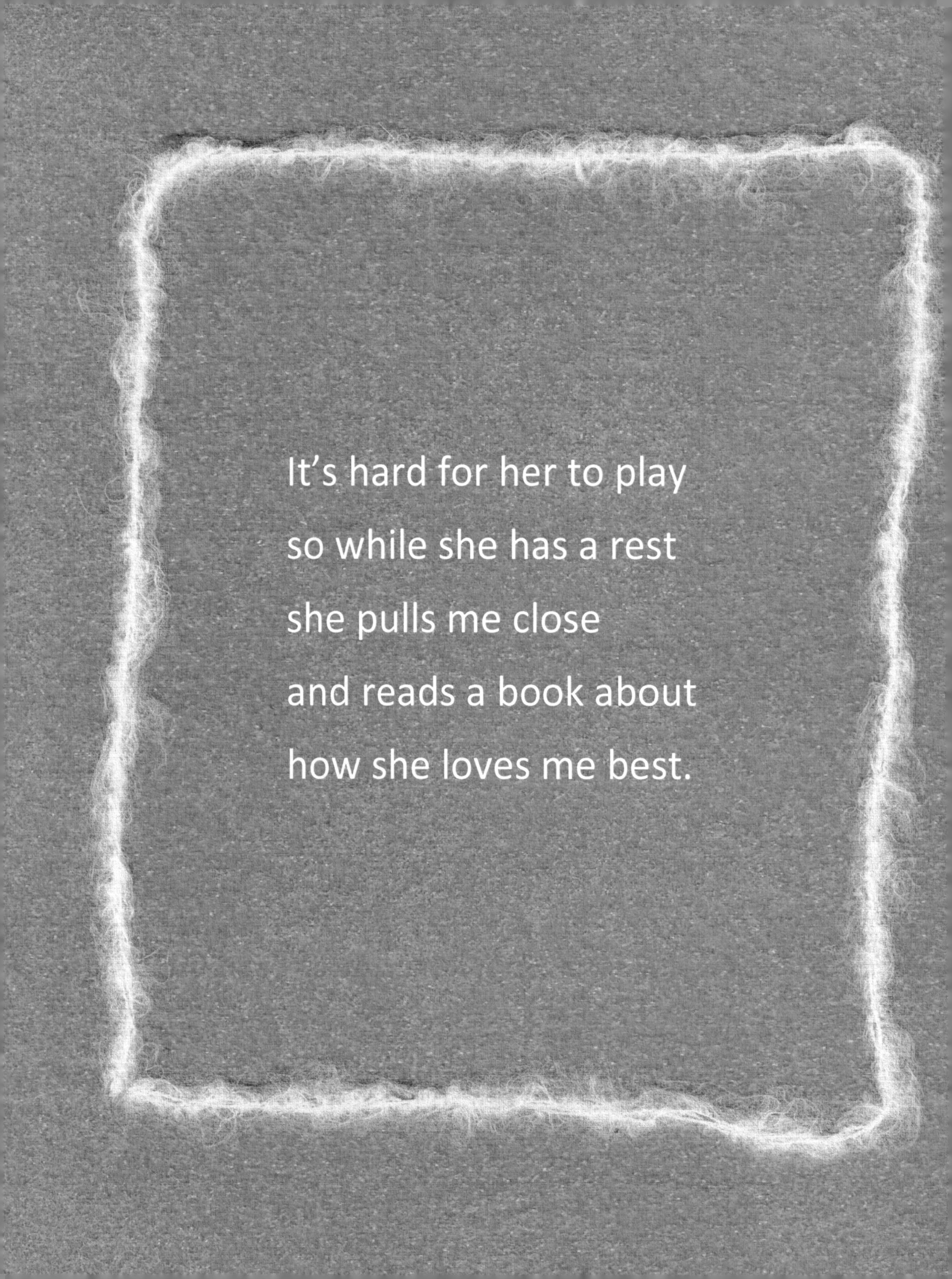

It’s hard for her to play
so while she has a rest
she pulls me close
and reads a book about
how she loves me best.

Elizabeth's Mommy had one baby

and Jacob's Mommy too

but MY Mommy is having two babies,

they will be here really soon!

Mommy will go to the hospital; the doctors will help get them out.

While she's gone I'll
play with Grandma,
there's excitement
all about!

Mom will sleep at the hospital; I can see my babies there.

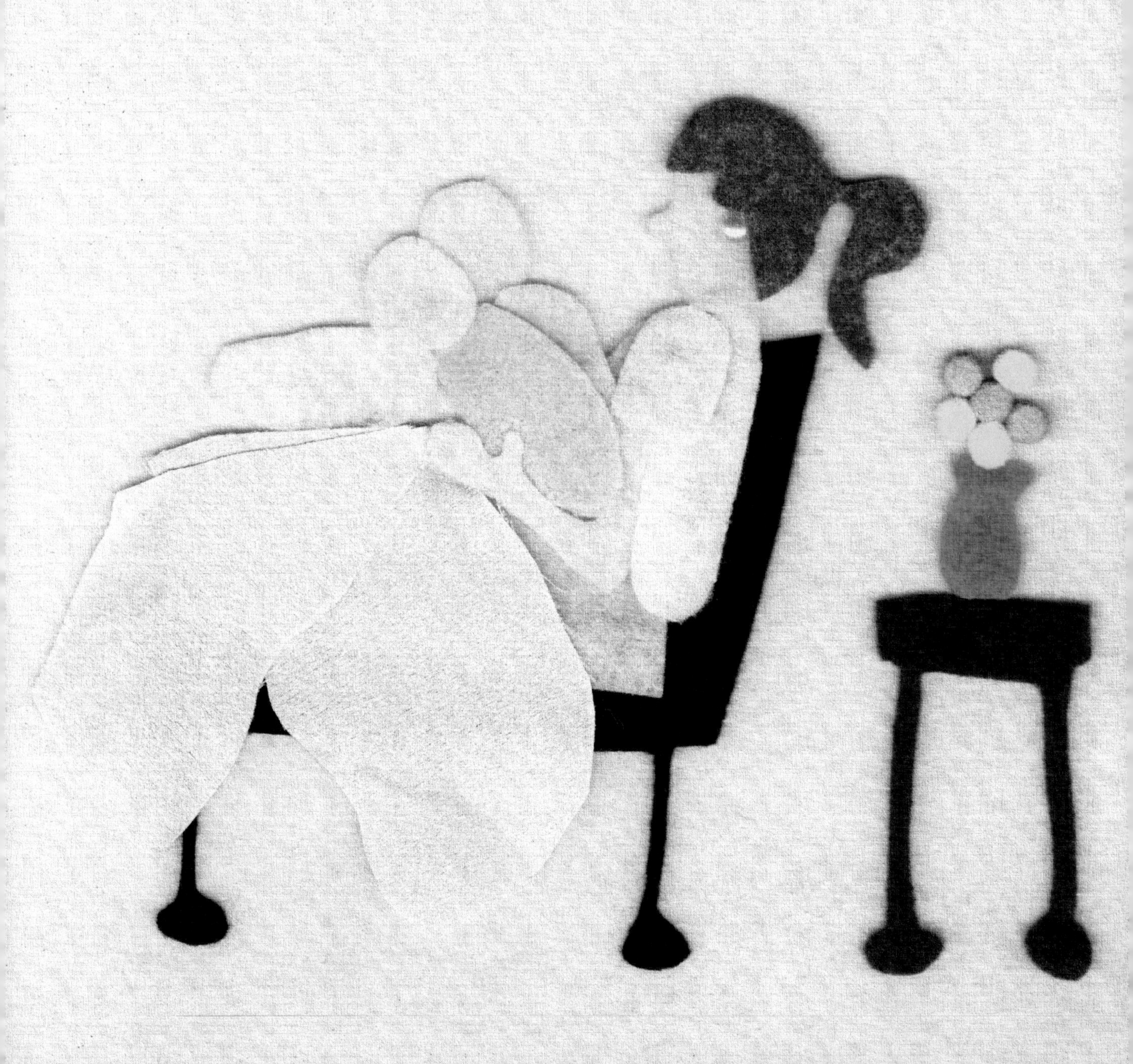

I’m now a proud big sister

I shout it everywhere!

Mom and the babies will come home

when each one is ready.

I’ll stroke their hair softly, Dad will hold them, keep them steady.

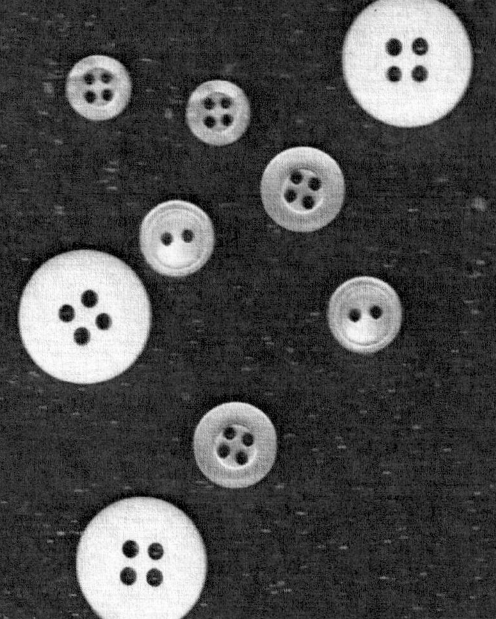

TWINS!

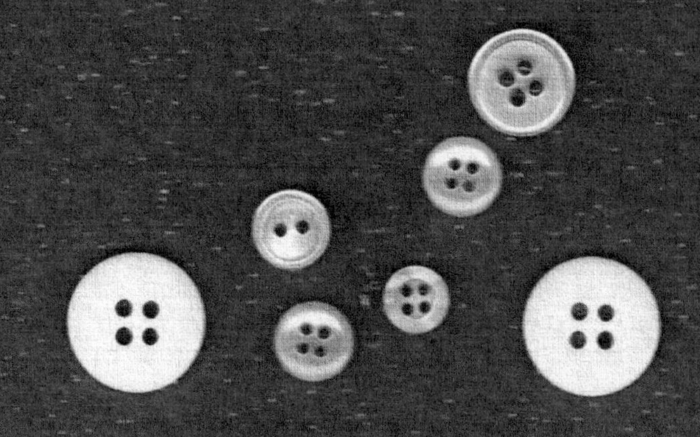

Two to feed

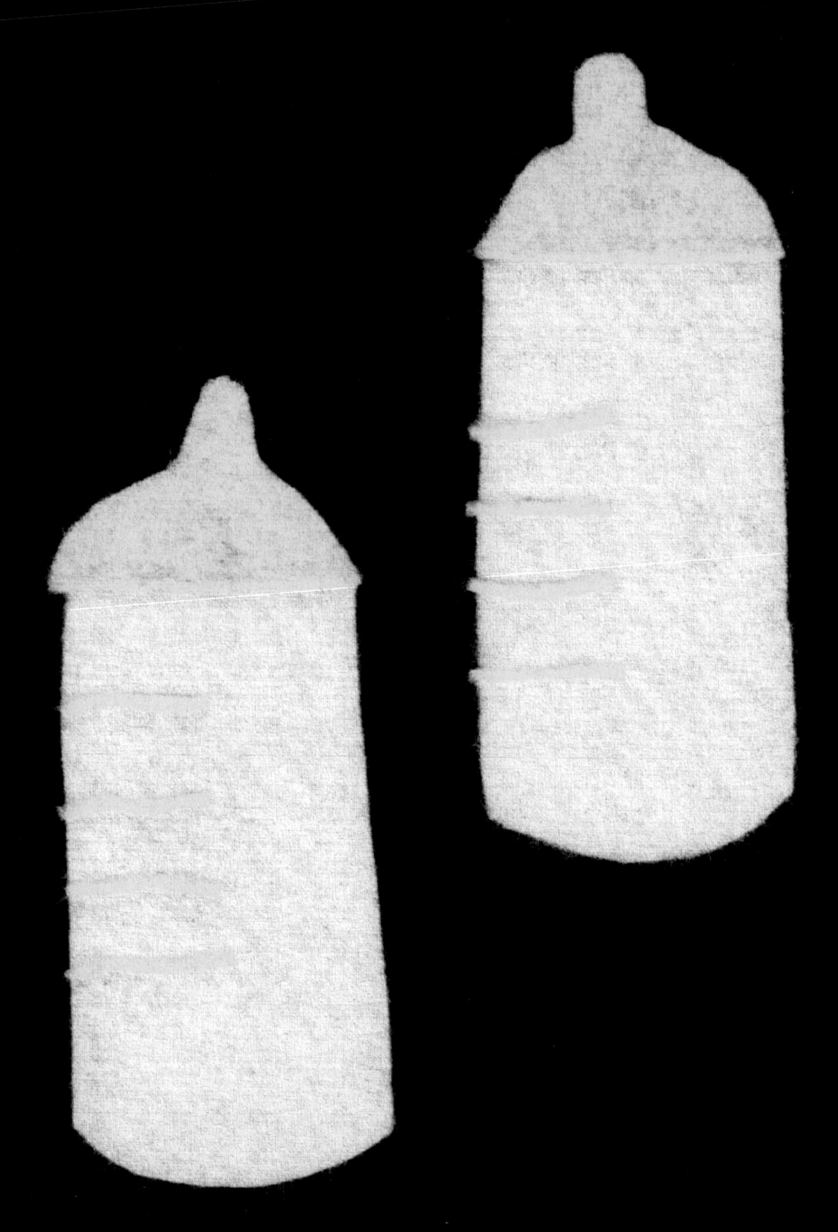

Two in the bath

Two in Mom and Daddy's lap.

Two babies need a lot of help;

I wonder when I can play?

Whee! Up I go, “It’s your turn now,”

I hear my Daddy say.

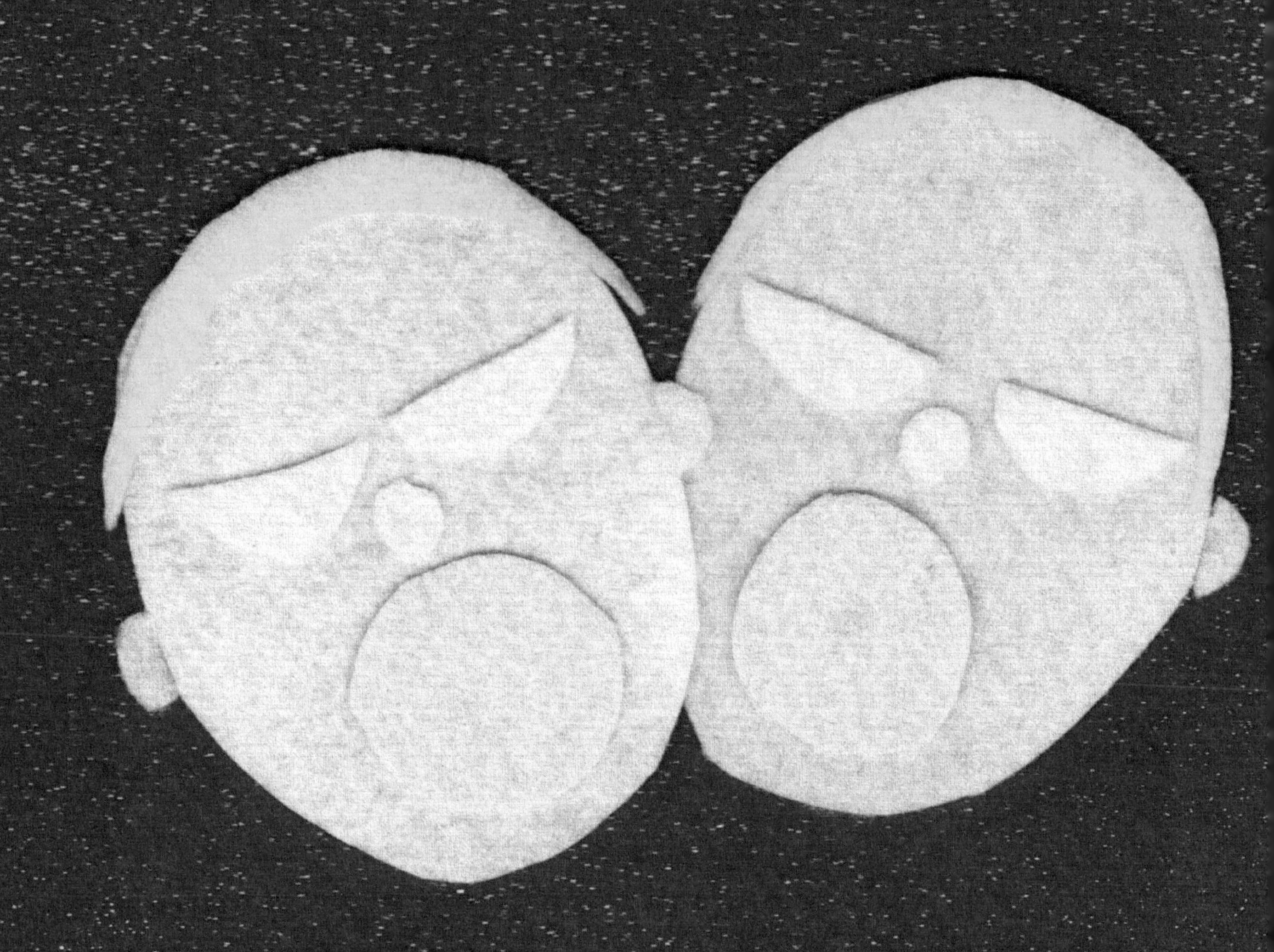

There's two babies crying now,

it quickly becomes loud.

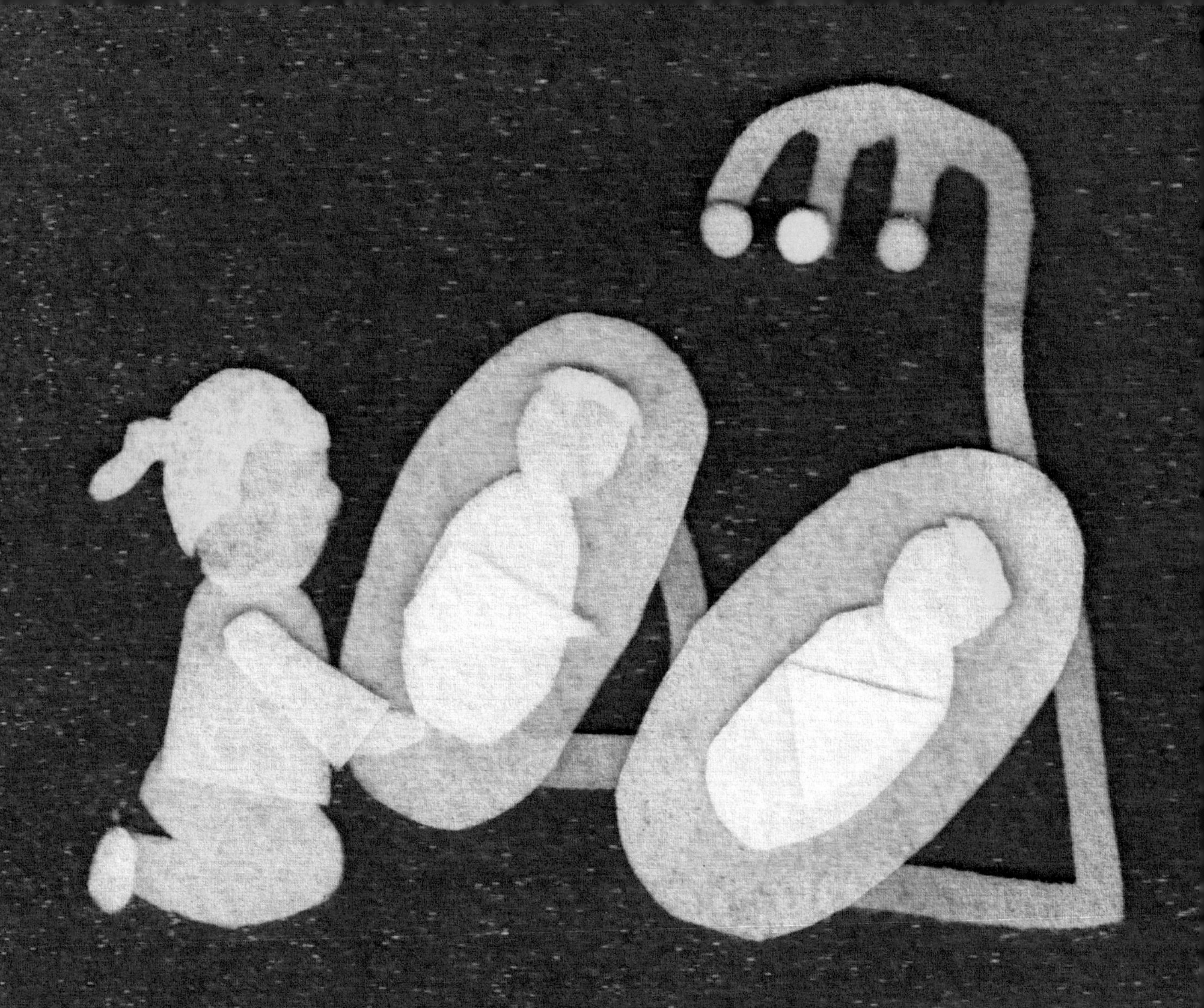

I can help Mom and Daddy
if I make quiet sounds.

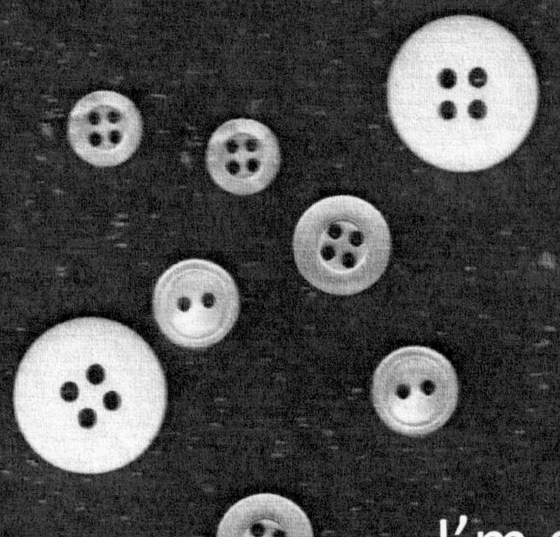

I’m so glad to know you
babies, hug and kiss you too.
I just want to say, I love you
babies, I’m glad I belong
to you!

THE END

ABOUT THE AUTHOR

Vivian occasionally climbs out of laundry piles to bring her stories of twin parenthood to life. As a mom to three her days cannot properly begin until she has had a dose of both lipstick and coffee. Forever the dreamer, she frequently imagines what she would do with a moment of solitude yet has never felt so deeply happy then right where she's at.

Thanks for following

IG @vivian_caldwell

www.viviancaldwell.com

Made in the USA
Middletown, DE
21 March 2019